RIKO RABBIT

by **Mei T. Nakano**

Cover and Illustrations
by **Chester H. Yoshida**

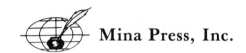 **Mina Press, Inc.**

Printed in the United States of America
Library of Congress Catalog Number 82-81737

ISBN 0-942610-00-8—Paperback

ISBN 0-942610-01-6—Hardcover

Mina Press Publishing Inc.
P.O. Box 162, Berkeley, CA 94701
P.O. Box 854, Sebastopol, CA 95472

586

FOR JASON AND KHALIL

Dear Reader,

I could not tell you this tale without telling you too that hundreds of years ago in Japan, an Empress bade a scribe write down a "historical record" of the creation of the world and of the events and successions of the line of Emperors and Empresses from the beginning of time. Myths, legends and songs, which had been passed down by word of mouth through the ages, were included in this "record," often interwoven into it. When this work, called the **Kojiki** *or "Record of Ancient Matters," was finished in 712 A.D., it filled three volumes. It is presently the oldest surviving Japanese book.*

I tell you all this because those tales of imagination in the **Kojiki** *have since inspired many literary works. One of them, a fable about a "white rabbit of Inaba," gave birth to the tale I am about to tell you.*

I am very grateful to that scribe who wrote down the fable, for he gave me the seeds of my story. But I am equally grateful to those ancient folks who had told the story in the beginning, who had joyously exercised their imaginations in telling and retelling it before it was written down. Each time they told it, I suspect, the rabbit became a slightly different character, and the story, of course, a different story.

I like to think that **Riko Rabbit** *came out of this storytelling tradition. Indeed, not long after Riko had romped through four or five pages of this book, he began to take on a life of his own. And I simply let him have his way.*

MTN

I

RAIN

A long time ago in Japan, there lived a rabbit. He was no ordinary rabbit, for he was covered with four inches of fine, soft fur which changed color with the seasons. In the warm season his fur was brown, the color of the rich earth. In the cold months it turned pure white to match the winter snow.

Nobody, not even the rabbit, knew for sure what made his coat change color. But his friends guessed that it was the rabbit himself who performed this marvel. *"Riko . . . riko . . ."* they would say nodding soberly when they saw that his coat had changed.

It was not long before the rabbit became known far and wide as Riko, Rabbit of Inaba. He was very proud of that name, for the word *riko* means "clever" in the country where he lived.

Riko's home was in a bamboo grove in a mountain village in Inaba. There, the slender, yellow and green bamboo grew in clumps on the gentle mountainside. The leaves from the bamboo which fell to the ground the year round became a thick, soft bed on which Riko and his friends could romp and chase about. They also liked to nibble on the tender, juicy bamboo shoots, which poked up out of the earth in the spring and summer. It was a happy place

8

to be.

Riko's favorite pastime, however, was to play tricks on his friends, then quickly run and hide. He thought this especially amusing since his friends could never find him. That, of course, was because he was the same color as the earth in the warm season and the same color as the snow in the cold season. This favorite trick made Riko seem more clever than ever to his friends. Riko himself could not help but believe that he must indeed be clever.

But one day something happened that would change his life forever.

It was summer. Riko had spent the morning playing with his friends as usual. And when he tired of that, he had stuffed himself with his favorite food of tender, juicy bamboo shoots. Soon afterwards, his eyes began to droop, and he settled down on the thick bed of leaves under a clump of bamboo.

He had been asleep for some time when he awoke with a sudden start.

9

Rain! It was raining!

Riko had been sleeping so soundly on his soft bed with his belly full of bamboo shoots that he had not even felt the raindrops. They had come slowly at first, but now they were falling in streaming sheets. Quickly he sprang up on his hind legs and looked about. He couldn't see anyone or anything through the blinding rain, only the dim shadow of the bamboo swinging low under the weight of the rain. Where had everyone gone?

Riko's breath came fast now, and his heart pounded. And as he felt himself sitting in a river of cold, rushing water, his eyes became round and frightened. Then before he could think what to do, he felt his hind legs slip out from under him.

"Yah!" he cried, at the same time clutching at a clump of bamboo nearby. "Help! Someone help!" he yelled again, but his voice did not even sound in his own ears. It was lost in the roaring rain.

A torrent of water rushed by and pulled at Riko's body, stretching it and causing him to lose his breath, but he clung to the clump of bamboo stubbornly.

Then all at once a great wave of water came roaring down the mountainside, and swept everything up in its path. The bamboo clump too, with Riko clinging to it, was jerked from its roots and whisked into the rushing torrent.

Riko clamped his eyes shut. At the same time, he held tightly to the clump of bamboo as if he were frozen to it. Head over heels and every which way, he tumbled down the mountainside, bumping hard against rocks and tree stumps. So frightened was he now that he could not shout for help. Nor did he feel any pain.

Then, quite suddenly, the tumbling seemed to stop, and Riko had a feeling that he had been carried to a high, soft bed, which was swaying gently to and fro.

"It must be a dream," he thought. He kept his eyes closed, hoping he would not wake up. But when moments passed by and the swaying did not stop, Riko opened his eyes slowly, carefully. What he saw made

his heart leap.

"Wah!" he shouted.

It was not a dream. The rushing waters had carried him and the bamboo clump down the mountainside and out to sea! The hollow stems of the bamboo, which were held fast by the tangled roots of the plant, formed a kind of boat that floated on the water.

Sitting on the little bamboo boat, Riko looked around at it, happy and amazed with himself. How clever he was to have clutched it all the way down the mountainside — especially since he could not swim!

Now he sat very still on the boat, not wanting to rock it. The storm had spent itself, and the rain fell gently. And even though his silky, brown fur was sopping wet, and his bones ached from the rocky ride, Riko felt good. He had, after all, not been seriously hurt and had saved himself from drowning. Surely he would think of something to rescue himself from the sea.

He knew it.

Sometime later it stopped raining altogether. The water gleamed under the bright sun.

Buka, buka. Buka, buka. The strange-looking boat floated on the water, bounced along by a gentle wind.

For a long time Riko traveled this way. His coat had long since dried, and he felt warm. But he was getting very tired and hungry and very, very lonely. At times he would stretch his eyes across the wide sea. He could see nothing but the blue-green water and the white foam of the gentle waves. At times he closed his eyes and imagined that he was at home in Inaba, frolicking about in the bamboo grove with his friends and stuffing himself with bamboo shoots. Finally he fell asleep.

How long he had been asleep he did not know, but a sudden jerk of the boat made his eyes pop open. For an instant it flashed across his mind that he was back in Inaba sleeping under the bamboo, and that one of his friends had shaken him to wake him. But no! When he looked up, there, directly in front of him, loomed a large, black rock. The boat had bumped into a large, black rock!

Riko rubbed his eyes. He could hardly believe it! The rock sat on the edge of a tiny island!

"Wah-h . . ." came a sound from him weakly. Riko stood up slowly, tottering, for his bones were cramped from the long boat ride. Then carefully he climbed up on the rock. There! He had saved himself again, he thought. Turning then to explore the island, Riko left the little bamboo boat bobbing up and down in the water.

II

A VISITOR

"It's so quiet on this island," Riko thought, looking around. "I wonder if anyone lives here."

Hopping off on his stiff, aching legs, he began to search the island. Poing-a, poing-a, back and forth he hopped. *"O-o-i!"* he would call loudly now and then. *"O-o-i!"* But there was no answer. He hopped back and forth for hours but found no one there.

19

Days passed. Plenty of herbs and grasses grew on the island so Riko did not go hungry. But he missed the tender, juicy bamboo shoots that poked out of the earth in the grove. Most of all he missed his friends there. *Ai-ii,* if he could only go back . . .

It was then that Riko remembered the bamboo boat. Quickly he ran to the rock upon which he had climbed when he came to the island and peered down into the water.

"The boat is gone . . ." he wailed aloud. "The boat is gone . . ."

Riko sat down slowly on the rock. Why hadn't he thought to save the boat, if he were so clever? How could he ever return home now?

His eyes stretched across the ocean. Clouds hung low in the sky there, and it seemed to him that they must be touching the bamboo grove in Inaba.

All at once tears welled up in his eyes. For the first time since he had been carried from his home, Riko felt truly alone in the world. His head sagged, and tears slid down his nose. He wiped his nose with his paws.

Just at that moment he thought he heard a splash out in the ocean. Yes! There it was again!

Riko jumped upright. Something dark was pushing itself up out of the water a short distance away. It looked like a large, black boat.

"Oya!" Riko's eyes brightened. His heart began to thump.

There was another splash.

"Yah! A crocodile!" he exclaimed. "Here! Over here, Wani San!" Riko called out. *"Wah-nee Sa-an!"* Over and over again he called, leaping back and forth on the rock and waving his arms. He was so excited he could not contain himself.

Finally the great crocodile caught sight of

Riko and turned to swim towards him. A large wave rolled as he swished his powerful tail to turn.

All Riko could see of the crocodile as he approached were his eyes and his nostrils. They seemed to be floating on the water towards him.

Shortly the great crocodile was very near the rock where Riko stood.

"Oy! Who are you?" he asked in a thundering voice.

Riko jumped back a little. "It's me, Riko of Inaba."

"Eh? Riko, is it? Riko, the clever rabbit of Inaba? Well, well." In spite of his thundering voice, the crocodile seemed friendly. When he spoke with his jaws wide open, he seemed to be smiling, though the sharp fourth teeth on the left and right sides of his lower jaw looked menacing.

"I am so happy to see you!" Riko said with a wide grin. "You see, I have been all alone here for a long time."

"Well, well," said the crocodile.

"And are you alone, Wani San?" Riko asked, looking around.

"Yes, today I am alone as you can see. Usually though, I travel about with my friends. I have many friends in this ocean."

"I have many friends too," Riko said, bobbing his head up and down. "But they live way over there in Inaba." He pointed across the ocean.

Then suddenly, like a bright light, an idea came to Riko.

"In fact, Wani San," he added, standing up straight and puffing out his chest, "in fact, I have so many friends, I can hardly count them. I must have more friends than anybody—more than you too, I'm sure."

"Wha-at?" The great crocodile swished his tail against the water. "What?" he bellowed again. This time his wide jaws, with the menacing fourth teeth bared, did not seem to be smiling.

"I only said I thought I had more friends than you," Riko said, standing with his legs apart, his paws on his hips.

"Ho! What a silly thing to say! Ho, *ho!*" the crocodile roared. "And *you* are a silly rabbit! You cannot see them, of course, but my friends are all over the sea. Why, when we are all gathered together, we are like a moving island on the sea, a moving island of crocodiles!"

Riko scratched his head. "Hm. Is that so? Hm. Let me see. Ah! I'll tell you what. Let's have a counting match to see which one of us *does* have more friends."

"Indeed! And how would we go about doing that?"

"I have an idea," Riko said, smiling. "You gather your friends together, and line them up from here to across the ocean over there. I can jump across their backs then and count them. When I reach the shores of Inaba, I will gather all of my friends and have them line up on the ledges of the shore so you can count them. How does that sound?"

"Good. That sounds like a good idea. Well, well, then." With that the great crocodile swished his tail against the water to turn once again.

A huge wave slammed high against the rock and showered Riko's brown coat with a fine spray. Shiny little drops slid off his back and fell to the rock.

25

III

A BRIDGE
OF CROCODILES

The great crocodile moved his body around the water, calling: *"O-o-i! O-o-i! Listen, everyone! Gather around!"*

Soon the sea was full of crocodiles, large and small. The water churned and foamed as they swished their powerful tails.

"What is it? What is it?" they asked, one after another.

"It's a contest. We're going to have a contest," the crocodile answered, smiling and circling about. "Riko of Inaba over there wants to have a counting match. He wants to see which one of us has more friends. *He wants to see which one of us has more friends!*"

"*Wah, hah!*" the crocodiles roared, all with their fourth teeth bared. They moved in closer to get a good look at Riko.

Riko looked them over, in turn, and could not help but exclaim to himself: "*Yah!* It *is* an island of crocodiles!"

Then he shouted out as loudly as he could: "Listen! Listen, everybody! I shall have to count you, so please, will you form a line from here to there?" He pointed in the direction of Inaba. "Then I will jump across your backs and count you as far as you go."

The great crocodile nodded, and his friends began to form a ragged line across the sea, joking, and jostling one another.

But even before they had finished lining up, Riko began to hop across their backs, counting.

". . . four, five, six, seven . . ." he counted. Soon the crocodiles had formed a line as far as the eye could see.

Poing-a, poing-a, Riko hopped along. At first he counted carefully, but soon his legs flew faster and faster, and he lost exact count.

At length when he had said the number "one-hundred and twenty-seven," he looked up, panting. There, not too far away, was the rocky shore of Inaba. The crocodiles were lined up right to the shore.

Home! He would be home again, just as he had dreamed so many times. How clever he was to have saved himself again! Now his legs carried him faster than ever.

Shortly Riko came to the last crocodile. "At last!" he said to himself, gasping for breath. But before climbing up on the rocky ledge of the land of Inaba, he turned around to glance at the long bridge he had crossed. Seeing the crocodiles still lined up in a row across the sea, Riko suddenly began to laugh. He laughed and laughed, and could not seem to stop.

"Wah, hah, hah!" Tears streamed down his face. "It's—it's so funny!"

"What's so funny?" demanded the last crocodile, the one on which Riko was standing.

"Excuse me," Riko said, still laughing. "I can't help it! Well . . . I guess there's no harm in telling you now . . . hah, hah! The thing is . . . you see, I didn't really want a counting match. What I wanted was to get back here to Inaba . . ."

As he spoke these last words, Riko made a giant step that would land him on the shores of Inaba. But just as he did so, the last crocodile seized Riko's hind leg with his sharp teeth.

"*Ya-ah!*" Riko's laughter turned into a scream. "What are you *doing?* Let go-o!" he yelled, grabbing a bush that grew on the ledge.

31

In no time, other crocodiles, including the great crocodile, gathered round. "You tricked us, you wicked rabbit!" they shouted angrily. "No one should trick a crocodile!" Then one of them grasped Riko's fur by the neck.

"*Ai-ii!* Please . . . !" Riko pleaded, casting his eyes toward the great crocodile. "Please, Wani San, tell them to let go! I didn't mean any harm!"

The great crocodile spoke in his thundering voice: "Well, well, Riko of Inaba. It was not a friendly thing, nor a very clever thing, for you to play that silly trick. It *was* silly, of course. You see, if you had asked, we would have been glad to help you cross the sea to your home here. One of us could have carried you on his back easily."

That is all the great crocodile had to say to Riko. Giving his tail a powerful swish, he turned to his friends. "Let him go now," he said calmly, and swam away.

Immediately the last crocodile let go of Riko's leg. And Riko, without wasting a moment, sprang for the shore once again.

But this time, a terrible thing happened. A burning pain streaked down the length of his body.

"Ya-aah . . .!" he howled.

The crocodile who had her teeth clamped on Riko's fur by the neck had not yet let go. And Riko's coat had been ripped from him from shoulder to toe!

Free now, with his feet on his homeland at last, Riko was nevertheless miserable— naked, ashamed, and suffering horribly. Worst of all, he could not go back to his home in the bamboo grove.

He limped away from the shore as best he could, wailing softly. And in the gully near a sand hill, he huddled in the shade of a clump of reeds.

IV

THE FORTY BROTHERS

Some distance from the land of Inaba, lived forty brothers, all princes of their land. The youngest, called the Prince of Izumo, was said by everyone to be kind and wise.

Now it happened that the forty brothers were to set out for Inaba one day. There, they would seek the hand of the beautiful Princess Yagami. It was time for the

Princess to be married, and the Empress Mother had sent for the forty brothers. She had heard that they were handsome and clever.

So the forty brothers set out for Inaba, each carrying a fine gift for the Princess. They had not gone far when one of the princes turned to the youngest brother, the Prince of Izumo and said, "This gift is a bother. Here. You carry it." With that, he put his gift in the young Prince's knapsack.

No sooner had he done this than another brother demanded that the Prince carry his gift too. One after another, each of the thirty-nine brothers put his gift into the Prince's knapsack. Then they strode merrily down the road towards Inaba without another care.

The Prince of Izumo, loaded down with the heavy bundle, lagged farther and farther behind. Soon he lost sight of his brothers.

37

The brothers had traveled some way when one of them complained: "I'm tired. Let's have a rest here before we go on into the village."

They had reached the seashore, and all the brothers agreed that it would indeed be a good place to rest. Before long, the lulling sounds of the water lapping against the shore, made the brothers begin to doze off, one after another.

But all at once, one brother sat up straight. "What is *that?*"

Others sat up too. "Eh?"

"That queer noise. What is it?"

"*Ai-ii . . . itaii . . .*" came a thin cry a short distance away.

"*Oya!*" the eldest brother exclaimed loudly. "It's coming from there!" He pointed in the direction of the sand hill as he said this, and sprang towards it.

Wide awake now, the other brothers followed close on his heels. When they came to the sand hill, they saw a small pink and red thing hiding under the reeds. One of its long ears dangled forward.

"Ho! What have we *here!*" Elder Brother said, half laughing.

"It looks like a rabbit," said another brother, lifting up Riko's dangling ear. "And look! It doesn't have a hair on its body!"

"Maybe it was just born!" joked another. At that, everyone laughed. And one after another, they continued making jokes.

Riko wished with all his heart that they would go, and leave him alone in his misery. Finally he could bear it no longer. "I can't help it . . ." he said in a faint voice. "They ripped off my coat."

"*Oya,* it speaks!"

"They ripped off your coat? Who are *they?*"

"The crocodiles."

"The crocodiles? Ah . . . the crocodiles!

You should know better than to fool with crocodiles. They are bad fellows."

Riko shook his head weakly. "No, no . . . it's not that. The thing is . . . the thing is — " He looked up at the thirty-nine brothers who had gathered round him. Then he suddenly decided to tell them what happened.

It took him a long time to tell. He told them about the rainstorm and how he had been washed to sea. He told them about the bamboo boat, and about landing on the island all alone. Then he told them about meeting the great crocodile and his friends and how he had tricked them into forming the bridge across the sea.

When he had at last finished his story, Riko was very tired. "So — that is how I came to be as I am."

"Indeed!" the eldest brother remarked. "Eh, you are a clever one, aren't you? But listen," he added, looking around at his brothers and grinning. "Listen, I can tell you how to get well. See that small rock pool over there? Plunge yourself into it. Then let the wind and sun dry you off. You will be very surprised at the result."

The other brothers grinned too. "We have to go now," one of them said. "We're off to win a princess! But don't forget what Elder Brother has told you!" Then laughing and joking still, the thirty-nine brothers went on their way.

Not long after they had disappeared down the road, Riko pulled his strength together and began to make his way down to the rocky pool. "In spite of their teasing, they wanted to help me, after all," he thought. Still, he was glad they had gone.

When he reached the pool, Riko plunged into it just as Elder Brother had advised.

"*Ai-iii!*" A piercing scream escaped his mouth. The salt water washing over his raw skin had made the pain worse, so much so that he could not bear it. As quickly as he had plunged in, he climbed out.

"Maybe this pain is good for me," he thought. "Maybe it will heal my skin and make my fur grow back." But when he let the sun and wind dry his skin, the pain grew even worse. Riko felt as though he were being burned alive. Hot tears welled up in his eyes. Then with great effort, he made his way back to the cool shade of the reeds beside the sand hill. Once more, he huddled there.

Presently he heard footsteps approaching, faintly at first, but now very near the spot where he huddled.

The footsteps belonged to the Prince of Izumo, the youngest of the forty brothers. Having been loaded down with the heavy bundle of gifts, he had lagged far behind the others. And now, as he was about to pass by the clump of reeds, something caught his eye. Laying down his bundle, he drew close to the strange object.

"Oya . . .!" he exclaimed softly. "It's a rabbit!" He bent over for a closer look. "My friend," he said to Riko, "what happened?"

Riko did not answer.

"Do not be afraid. I am the Prince of Izumo. Tell me what happened so I can help you."

Still Riko did not answer.

"Please. I can see that you are in pain. You must let me help you quickly, for I must be on my way. What is your name, my friend?"

After a moment Riko looked up. The face he saw was very much like the voice he had heard—kind and gentle. Then weakly, he uttered, "Riko . . . my name is Riko."

"Ah. I have heard of you Riko. The clever rabbit of Inaba."

Again Riko did not answer. Once he had been proud of being called "the clever rabbit of Inaba," but now, somehow, he wanted to cast off that name.

"But tell me, quickly. What happened to you?"

Then because the young prince seemed so kind, Riko told him the whole miserable story from beginning to end.

"Hmm," said the Prince when Riko had finished. "That is quite a story. So you played a clever trick on the crocodiles, and they took your precious coat away. Then my brothers came along and played a cruel joke on you. It *was* a joke, I'm afraid. That is why you are in such misery."

Riko said nothing. He just sat very still, blinking his eyes rapidly.

"But look here, do not look so sad. You will recover," the Prince promised. "Here is what you must do. First, bathe yourself in that stream over there. It flows down from the mountain, and is fresh and sweet. It will not hurt you like the salt water from the sea. And here, take these cattails from the reeds and open up the brown spikes. Inside, you will find a soft, silky down. Wrap your whole body in the down. Then rest in the shade until the pain disappears."

When he had finished speaking, the Prince picked up his large bundle, heaved it to his shoulders, and turned to go.

"Please," Riko said, "can't you stay a little longer?"

"I wish I could, Riko of Inaba," the Prince replied. "But I must hurry, as I said before. I must deliver these gifts to the palace. My brothers and I seek the hand of the beautiful Princess Yagami, and I must get there before it is time for the Princess to receive us. Perhaps we will meet when you are well and strong. Goodbye then, my friend."

Riko watched the Prince go down the path with his large bundle on his back. Then he went down to the stream and stuck his foot in it uncertainly. The water felt cool and good, so he sat down in it and bathed

himself. How soothing it was to his burning skin!

After that, he wrapped himself in the blanket of silky down he had gotten from inside the brown spikes of the cattails. The pain began to disappear almost at once. And as he lay in the shade of the tall reeds, Riko knew that he would recover. Silently he thanked the good Prince.

Many days passed. Little by little, Riko's fur began to grow in until, one day, his entire body was once more covered with a soft coat. This time, the coat was pure white, for winter was approaching.

V

THE PRINCESS

The thirty-nine brothers had arrived at the palace some time ago. Now bathed and rested, they were seated in the Receiving Chamber outside the Great Hall, waiting to be received by Princess Yagami. They sat on the floor along three walls of the Chamber. Food and drink lay on the small tables lined up before them. As they ate and drank, their voices grew merrier and

49

louder. Mostly, they joked about the rabbit of Inaba.

". . . Hah, hah, ha-ah! A truly fine joke!" one brother was saying, as he lifted his cup in the air.

Another brother, slapping his lap, said, ". . . Telling that clever rabbit to jump into the sea . . . ! Wo, ho! Who thought of that one?"

"Now instead of calling him the clever rabbit of Inaba, we should call him the *hairless* wonder of Inaba!" joked another.

That made the Chamber rock with laughter.

In the midst of this uproar, the Prince of Izumo entered the Chamber. Walking to the center of the room, he set his heavy bundle down. A hush fell on the Chamber.

"Here are the gifts," the Prince said. "I see that I have delivered them in time."

"Just be glad you *did!*" shouted a brother roughly. "Why are you so late?"

51

The Prince looked at him and did not answer.

"Well, never mind any excuses!" another brother scolded. "Go and clean yourself. You look like a beggar!"

Then the brothers turned back to their merrymaking.

Before long, a message came that the Princess was ready to receive them. The forty brothers filed quietly through the sliding-panel doors, their faces sober now. They entered the Great Hall and sat in rows on the rice-straw mats that covered the gleaming, wooden floor.

Princess Yagami sat before them on a red, silk pillow. Her straight, black hair, glistening and beautiful, flowed down over the back of her purple kimono and touched the red pillow. The Empress Mother sat beside her.

The Empress spoke. "We know you have come a long way," she said in a clear, strong

voice. "For that, we thank you. We hope you have rested well and have had something to refresh yourselves."

All the brothers bowed.

"Now my daughter wishes to speak."

Princess Yagami bowed her head ever so slightly. "I am afraid we have something unpleasant we must say," she said. Her voice was like a bird's, light and musical, but her eyes were dark and serious.

"We speak to all of you except the youngest, who is called the Prince of Izumo, we are told." She unclasped her hands on her lap, then clasped them again. "You have brought many gifts for us we understand, and I must tell you that we cannot accept them now. Nor can we receive your offers of marriage. You see, we have heard that you were not even willing to carry your own gifts here, and that you thoughtlessly loaded them on your brother's back."

"Yes," the Empress Mother said sharply. "Have you not heard the old saying 'He who would call himself a lantern-bearer should bear his own lantern'? Furthermore, we have also heard of your cruel joke on poor Rabbit of Inaba. Had not your brother kindly stopped to help him, he might lay dying at this very moment. Because of your cruel misdeeds, our daughter will cut off her hair. This will make it very unlikely that anyone will speak for her hand, but that cannot be helped.

The brothers stirred and cast sidelong glances at one another before looking down again.

"Eh? You are surprised?" The Empress' voice was stern. "Do you not know that we must all answer for one another? And that when harm is done, someone must pay, often an innocent one?"

She looked slowly around at each of the faces. "Now, if you have nothing to say, I must ask you to leave the palace. And please take your gifts with you. The youngest of you may stay if he wishes."

Without a sound, the thirty-nine brothers rose and bowed. Heads lowered, they filed silently out of the Great Hall.

Alone before the Princess and her mother now, the Prince of Izumo sat, head bowed, leaning forward slightly. The palms of his hands pressed down hard on each folded knee.

VI

RIKO'S GIFT

In Inaba snow covered the ground, for it was winter.

Riko had long ago returned to the bamboo grove in the village. Now he was covered with four inches of fur as white as snow. His friends still admired his beautiful coat, though they no longer called him "the clever rabbit of Inaba". Riko had asked them to forget that name.

One morning, when the sun was glistening on the snow, the great bell of the village temple sounded.

"Why is the temple bell ringing?" Riko asked, for it was not ringing at the usual hour. Riko knew that sometimes the bell rang on a special day — a sad day or a happy day.

"It's a happy day! Haven't you heard?" one of Riko's friends shouted. "The bell is ringing the news that the beautiful Princess Yagami is to be wed to the Prince of Izumo!"

Riko let out a gasp. So! It *was* a happy day! The Princess was said to be as kind as she was beautiful, and Riko was very glad that she had chosen the Prince to be her husband.

Many times, Riko had thought of the Prince's great kindness to him. And many times, he had wished he could show the Prince how grateful he was. He wished too that he could show the Prince how his beautiful white coat had grown back again. And now that this happy day was to come for the Prince and the Princess, Riko wished more than anything that he could find a way to tell them that he was happy too.

But what could he do? If he were rich, he could buy a fine wedding present. If he were wise, he could give them a wise and lasting thought. And if he were just big and strong, he could cut down a cedar tree, and build a handsome chest for the married couple.

But Riko knew he was none of these things, and in the end he would have to depend on himself as he was—plain Riko, Rabbit of Inaba.

Then an idea slowly took form in his head. He thought about it for days and days. Finally, he came up with a plan that would work. Yes, it would work!

The next day, he turned to his friend.

"Will you help me?" he asked. "I want to cut off my fur, but I cannot do it alone. Please take this sharp stone and help me cut it."

"*What?*" Riko's friend could hardly believe his ears.

"Please," Riko repeated. "I am asking you to help me cut off my fur."

"I can't do that, you silly rabbit!" his friend said in horror. "You will freeze to death in this cold! Isn't that right?" He turned to the other rabbits who had gathered about.

"Of course! Of course!" they all agreed.

"But really, it will be all right," Riko assured them. "Since we stay indoors in the winter anyway, I could share the warmth of your coats—if you will let me. You see, I must have the fur for a wedding present for the Prince and Princess."

Riko's friends were puzzled at the thought of fur for a wedding present, but they were willing to share the warmth of their coats.

So it was done. Riko's beautiful white coat was once again sheared off.

Then Riko made a square, sitting-pillow to cover with the white fur. For days and days, weeks and weeks, he worked on it, carefully sewing each hair into place. When

he finished at last, all his friends marveled at the beautiful pillow covered with silky, white fur. They thought it the finest pillow they had ever seen.

On the day of the wedding, the temple bells rang once again. Folks traveled from miles around to present their wedding gifts to the married couple, forming a long, curving line outside the palace. Even the thirty-nine brothers stood in line, each carrying a bale of rice on his shoulder.

When Riko finally passed through the palace gates, it was almost nightfall. He did not enter the First Waiting Room as the others had done.

"Excuse me," he said to one of the guards at the door. "Will you kindly put this with the other wedding gifts? I cannot go in, for I wear no sandals, and I am afraid my feet will soil the straw mats on the floor."

The guard nodded, and carefully carried the white pillow inside, bearing it on his outstretched arms.

The Prince and the Princess had received hundreds of fine wedding presents. And for days, they looked the presents over, delighted and thankful for each one. But when at last they came to the splendid white pillow, they both gasped.

"It is from Riko of Inaba! It is his coat of fur!" the Prince said.

"What a lovely, wonderful gift," the Princess said, as she stroked the rich, silky fur of the pillow.

Then the two spoke of how Riko must have shivered in the cold through the long winter without his coat, and their hearts were filled with gratitude for the great gift he had given them.

Suddenly, the Princess' eyes clouded over with tears. Her delicate hands went to the wig which covered her head and pushed an ornament in. "I gave up my hair because of your brothers' misdeeds. I wonder if Riko gave up his for something too."

"Yes, I am sure of it," the Prince said soberly. "His gift shall be our most treasured possession."

Riko had indeed shivered in the cold sometimes even though his friends had shared the warmth of their coats, true to their promise.

But now in the spring, with the sun beginning to warm the earth, Riko was already covered with an inch of silky, brown fur.

Book design by Shiro Nakano

This book was set in English Times by
Taber Type, Sebastopol, CA
Printed by West Coast Print Center, Berkeley, CA